Early Bird Stories: Early Bird Readers: Purple (Lerner Publicat   7/22/2019

 Four Little Pigs   **$20.99**

Tom's granny is a witch! When he tells her that the Three Little Pigs is boring, Granny uses her magic to send him into the book. Now Tom must beware of the big bad wolf!

#2115006   K. Nye   Available:08/01/2019   32 pgs
Grade:K12   Dewey:E

Great Grizzly Race   **$20.99**

A mean bear has stolen all the bikes before the big race. The Dog Detectives must find the bikes and stop the bully from cheating his way to the finish line!

#2115007   Z. Lumsden   Available:08/01/2019   32 pgs
Grade:K12   Dewey:E

Grumpy King Colin   **$20.99**

King Colin is naughty, lazy, silly, and grumpy. But he is king, so he'll do what he wants! But he'll discover that even a king can't get away with everything . . .

#2115008   P. Allcock   Available:08/01/2019   32 pgs
Grade:K12   Dewey:E

 Hocus Pocus Diplodocus   **$20.99**

Hocus P. Diplodocus is not like other dinosaurs. He is the world's first magician! But as Hocus's powers grow, his fame grows too, and everything could go very wrong!

#2115009   S. Howson   Available:08/01/2019   32 pgs
Grade:K12   Dewey:E

EARLY BIRD
STORIES

A Royal Mess

Early★Reader

First American edition published in 2019 by Lerner Publishing Group, Inc.

An original concept by Rachel Lyon
Copyright © 2020 Rachel Lyon

Illustrated by Catalina Echeverri

First published by Maverick Arts Publishing Limited

Maverick
arts publishing

Licensed Edition
A Royal Mess

Lerner Publications Company
A division of Lerner Publishing Group, Inc.
241 First Avenue North
Minneapolis, MN 55401 USA

For reading levels and more information, look up this title at www.lernerbooks.com.

Main body text set in Mikado. Typeface provided by HVD Fonts.

Library of Congress Cataloging-in-Publication Data

Names: Lyon, Rachel, 1978– author. | Echeverri, Catalina, 1986- illustrator.
Title: A royal mess / by Rachel Lyon ; illustrated by Catalina Echeverri.
Description: Minneapolis : Lerner Publications, [2019] | Series: Early bird readers. Purple (Early bird stories) | "The original picture book text for this story has been modified by the author to be an early reader." | Originally published in Horsham, West Sussex by Maverick Arts Publishing Ltd. in 2017.
Identifiers: LCCN 2018043866 (print) | LCCN 2018052764 (ebook) | ISBN 9781541561717 (eb pdf) | ISBN 9781541542280 (lb : alk. paper)
Subjects: LCSH: Readers (Primary) | Rabbits—Juvenile literature. | Friendship—Juvenile literature. | Thoughtfulness—Juvenile literature.
Classification: LCC PE1119 (ebook) | LCC PE1119 .L866 2019 (print) | DDC 428.6/2—dc23

LC record available at https://lccn.loc.gov/2018043866

Manufactured in the United States of America
1-45402-39036-10/24/2018

EARLY BIRD STORIES

A Royal Mess

Rachel Lyon

Illustrated by
Catalina Echeverri

Lerner Publications ◆ Minneapolis

Queen Fluff was a very fancy bunny.

The Royal Burrow

She always wore a big fancy crown,

and lived in a big fancy burrow.

Even though she had plenty of money,

Queen Fluff had no friends at all.

Not one. She was lonely and bored.

One day she had an idea. "I will go and visit all the bunnies in my kingdom," she said. "When I find the bunny with the fanciest burrow, I'll stay with them for a week."

So Queen Fluff sent a letter to every bunny in the kingdom. She ordered them to make their burrows fancy and to cook her a fancy feast.

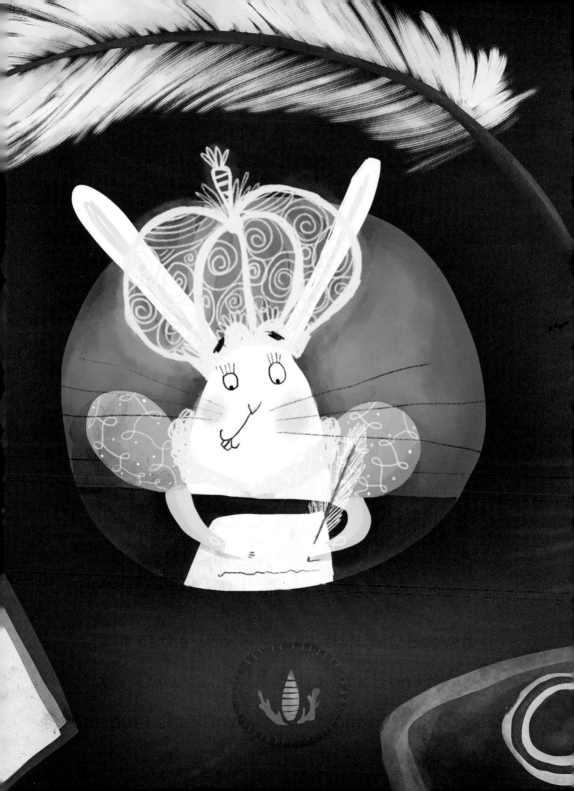

Bunnyshire

But the other bunnies in
the kingdom were poor.
They couldn't afford
fancy things.

"Queen Fluff must be very thoughtless," they said.
"Let's teach her a lesson!" So the bunnies worked
very hard, getting ready for the queen's visit.

They collected all the smelliest, yuckiest things they
could find. They put all the smelly, yucky things in
their burrows.

The queen was busy too, getting ready for her trip. She couldn't wait to see the other bunnies' burrows and choose which was the fanciest.

The Royal Burrow

Bunnyshire

When the big day came, she set off in her fancy
royal coach.

When the bunnies saw her arrive, they giggled. What would the queen think of their messy, smelly burrows?

The queen ran eagerly into the first burrow.

But the only thing
waiting for her was
a swarm of bees!

"Yawoooh!" she yelped,
as the bees stung her
on her furry bottom.
"That's no way to treat
a queen!"

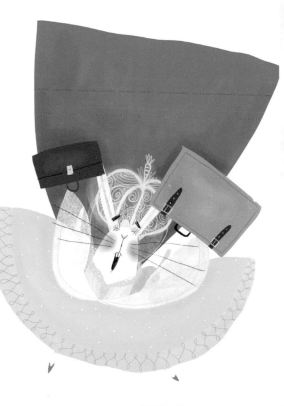

The next burrow was even worse!
It was full of toads and creepy-crawlies.

"Some lunch, my lady?" asked the bunnies
inside, offering her a bowl of slug soup.

"Yuck!" said the queen, and she ran right
off to the next burrow.

Plop! The queen slid down into the burrow, and landed in a big pile of muck!

"My shiny gold slippers are ruined!"

she wailed.

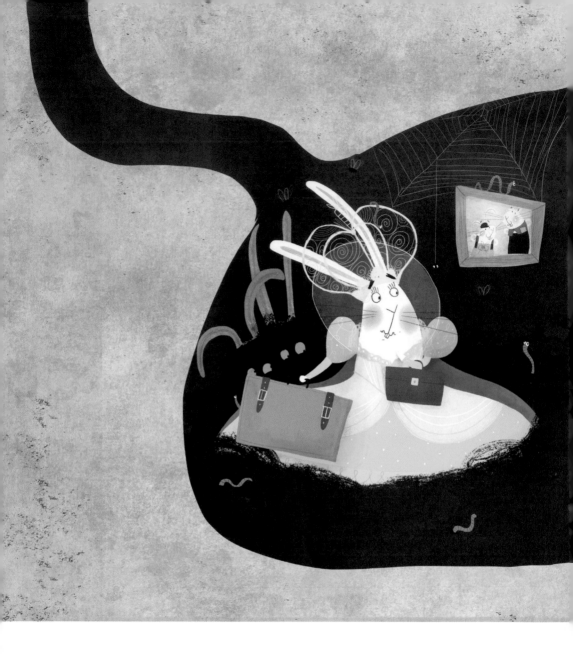

There was no one there to greet her except for

a rat . . . who was wearing only his underpants!

Queen Fluff was fed up. "I'm leaving!" she cried.

"Hooray!" cheered the bunnies. "We did it!

We got rid of thoughtless Queen Fluff!"

But the queen had heard every word they said.

"Oh dear," said Queen Fluff, taking off her crown.

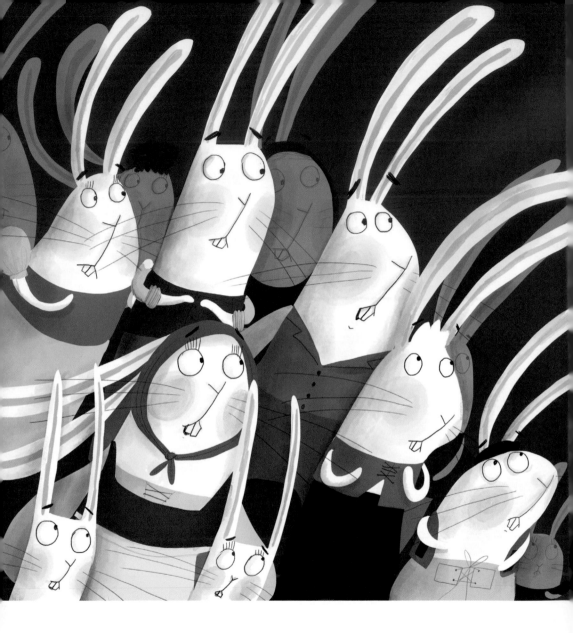

"I see now. You're right—I have been
thoughtless and unkind. If only there was
a way we could be friends."

Suddenly the queen had an idea. "I know! Why don't you come back to my place for a party?" she said.

That night, as the bunnies danced and laughed and ate together . . .

Queen Fluff realized that although fancy burrows and fancy feasts are nice, real friends are far nicer.

Quiz

1. Why is Queen Fluff unhappy?

   a) She has lost her birthday cake.

   b) Her fancy dress was ruined.

   c) She has no friends.

2. What does Queen Fluff want to find?

   a) The fanciest burrow

   b) A new crown

   c) A gold slipper

3. Why do the other bunnies want to trick Queen Fluff?

   a) Because they think she is thoughtless

   b) Because they want to sleep in her burrow

   c) Because they want to eat her carrots

4. What does Queen Fluff find in the burrows?

   a) Gold crowns

   b) Smelly, yucky things

   c) Fancy parties

5. How does Queen Fluff become friends with the other bunnies?

   a) She buys them all new burrows.

   b) She cooks them a feast.

   c) She invites them to a party.

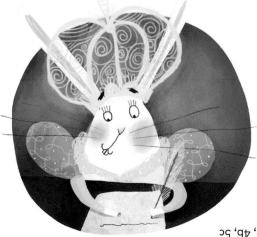

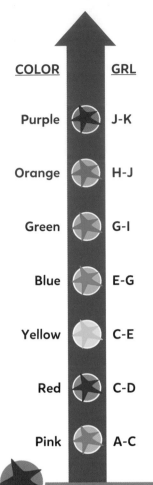

COLOR		GRL
Purple		J-K
Orange		H-J
Green		G-I
Blue		E-G
Yellow		C-E
Red		C-D
Pink		A-C

EARLY BIRD STORIES

Leveled for Guided Reading

Early Bird Stories have been edited and leveled by leading educational consultants to correspond with guided reading levels. The levels are assigned by taking into account the content, language style, layout, and phonics used in each book.